Airy Fairy

Magic Music!

Look out for more stories...

Magic Music!

Margaret Ryan
illustrated by Teresa Murfin

BARRON'S

To Rosalyn, with love

First edition for the United States, the Philippines, and Canada published by Barron's Educational Series, Inc., 2006

First published by Scholastic Ltd, 2005

Text copyright © Margaret Ryan, 2005
Illustrations copyright © Teresa Murfin, 2005

The right of Margaret Ryan and Teresa Murfin to be identified as the author and illustrator of this work respectively has been asserted by them in accordance with the Copyright, Designs and Patents Act, 1988.

All inquiries should be addressed to:
Barron's Educational Series, Inc.
250 Wireless Boulevard
Hauppauge, New York 11788
www.barronseduc.com

Library of Congress Control Card No. 2005930767

ISBN-13: 978-0-7641-3427-2
ISBN-10: 0-7641-3427-2

Printed in China
9 8 7 6 5 4 3 2

Chapter One

It was Monday morning at Fairy Gropplethorpe's Academy for Good Fairies and Airy Fairy was getting ready for school. She pulled on her pink fairy dress as she sang along to Freddie Sprite on the radio.

"I am flying. I am flying
Over fields and oceans, too.
I am flying, flip-flap flying.
Soon I'll be there, close to you."

Macduff and Rainbow, who had been asleep on top of her school socks, shot under her bed and put their paws over their ears.

"What's the matter with you two?" said Airy Fairy. "Don't you like Freddie Sprite? I think he's great. He's my favorite pop star."

Macduff and Rainbow blinked but said nothing.

Then the bell rang for morning assembly and Airy Fairy quickly pulled on her warm socks, tied a neat bow on her pink sneakers, and flew downstairs.

"I don't want to be late," she muttered, swerving to avoid twin fairies, Twink and Plink, who always flew together. "Miss Stickler gets very annoyed when I'm late." But she got into the assembly hall in time.

"Hi Buttercup. Hi Tingle," she waved to her friends. "Good morning, Miss Stickler." She smiled at her teacher. Then she tripped over the laces of her sneakers, knocked over Miss Stickler, and sent the teacher's books flying everywhere.

"Oh, sorry, Miss Stickler," gasped Airy Fairy, trying to help her up and rescue the books at the same time. "I don't know how that happened. I was sure I had tied my laces."

Miss Stickler took the books from Airy Fairy and frowned.

"Not a good start to the week, Airy Fairy," she said. "Not a good start at all. Now go and sit down and try to behave."

"Yes, Miss Stickler. Sorry, Miss Stickler," sighed Airy Fairy, and went to sit beside Buttercup and Tingle. Scary Fairy, sitting behind them, immediately poked her with her wand.

"Enjoy your trip?" she giggled.

Airy Fairy poked her right back. "I should have known it was you up to your dirty tricks," she said. "I knew I had tied my laces."

"Airy Fairy!" Miss Stickler was really angry. "Turn around and stop poking poor Scary Fairy. It's first thing on a Monday morning and already you're in trouble. There will be extra homework for you tonight."

Airy Fairy sighed. It was always the same. Scary Fairy, who was Miss Stickler's niece, always was up to rotten tricks, but Airy Fairy always was the one who got caught.

"Never mind, Airy Fairy," whispered Buttercup and Tingle. "We'll help you with the homework."

"Thank you," whispered Airy Fairy, and stood up as Fairy Gropplethorpe arrived.

Fairy Gropplethorpe waved all the fairies to their seats. "Good morning, Fairies," she beamed, "and welcome to the start of another week. And what a week it's going to be. I have exciting news. This week we're having a special guest. My friend, Fairy Glissando, is coming to visit us."

"Not Fairy Glissando, the famous musician!" cried Honeysuckle.

"She's fantastic," said Silvie.

"She can play anything," said Skelf.

Fairy Gropplethorpe smiled. "She certainly can, and I thought it would be nice to put on a little concert to welcome her. Then, who knows, she might choose one of you to play something with her."

"She might just do that," said Miss Stickler. "Some of our fairies are very musical."

"I can play the triangle," said Tingle.

"I can play 'Three Blind Mice' on the recorder," said Buttercup.

"And we can play 'Chopsticks' on the old school piano when the keys don't stick down," said Twink and Plink.

"Huh, that's nothing," boasted Scary Fairy. "I am just like Fairy Glissando. I can play anything on any instrument I choose."

"That's true," Miss Stickler beamed at her niece. "Scary Fairy is very gifted."

Airy Fairy gnawed at a fingernail and worried.

I can't play anything, she thought, *and I don't think Macduff and Rainbow even liked my singing. Perhaps I could just turn the pages for the others.*

But Fairy Gropplethorpe had other ideas.

"I want everyone to be able to play something for Fairy Glissando, even if it's not perfect. It's trying hard that's important. I still have to try hard at some things, too. I tried hard at some musical spells over the weekend and look what I managed to do."

And Fairy Gropplethorpe swished back the stage curtain behind her and stood aside.

Everyone gasped. There, gleaming in the morning sunshine, stood a fine collection of musical instruments. A fat cello puffed importantly beside some violins. A French horn towered over several trumpets, while a long, skinny trombone stood haughtily on its own, ignoring the little keyboard standing nearby.

"Well, Fairies," beamed Fairy Gropplethorpe. "What do you think of those?"

"Awesome," said Skelf.

"Fantastic," said Cherri.

"When can we try them?" asked Silvie.

"We'll begin right away," said Fairy Gropplethorpe. "You'll need lots of practice, but do your best and Fairy Glissando is sure to be impressed by your efforts."

"I'll try really hard," said Honeysuckle.

"We'll try really, really hard," breathed Twink and Plink.

"I'll try as hard as I can," whispered Airy Fairy to Buttercup and Tingle. "But I can't play anything at all. I'll probably be hopeless as usual."

"Just do your best and you'll be fine," soothed her friends.

"Oh no, you won't," muttered Scary Fairy, listening in. "I'll soon see to that. I'm the cleverest fairy in this school AND the most musical. Fairy Glissando is going to be impressed by me. Only me."

Chapter Two

Fairy Gropplethorpe left the assembly hall and Miss Stickler went up onto the platform.

"Now, Fairies," she said. "Pay attention. I want you to try out all the instruments Fairy Gropplethorpe has magicked up, to see which one is best for you. We don't have long to learn how to play them, but if you all work very hard," and she looked very hard at Airy Fairy, "I'm sure you will succeed."

But Airy Fairy wasn't so sure.

"Just look at the size of that cello," she said to Buttercup and Tingle. "I don't think I could lift it, never mind play it. And that French horn looks very bad-tempered. I wonder why it's called a French horn. Did it come all the way from France? I wonder if you can get Spanish horns, or Portuguese horns, or even Outer Mongolian horns. I think Outer Mongolian goats have horns, but I don't know if you can play them..."

"Airy Fairy, do be quiet, and come up here and choose an instrument," said Miss Stickler.

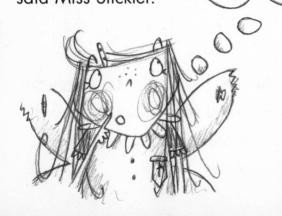

"Yes, Miss Stickler. Sorry, Miss Stickler,"
said Airy Fairy, and flew up onto the stage.

She looked at all the musical instruments.
They looked even scarier up close.

"I don't know which one to choose first,"
she muttered, fluttering around each one in
turn.

Miss Stickler heard her and handed her the
bow for the cello.

"Get a move on, Airy Fairy," she said.

Airy Fairy sat down on a chair and pulled the cello toward her.

"Hello, Mr. Cello," she whispered. "Is it all right if I pluck one of your strings?"

BOOOOONNNG.

"Aaaah!"

Airy Fairy frightened herself and fell off the chair.

The other fairies giggled. Miss Stickler frowned.

"Sorry, Miss Stickler," muttered Airy Fairy, and climbed back up again.

"I didn't think that would be so loud, Mr. Cello," she whispered. "Could you play more softly next time?" And she gently plucked another string.

Binnnnng.

"Oh, that's much better," said Airy Fairy. "I could try those two strings together now."

Binnnng. Bonnnng.

"That sounds nice, Airy Fairy," said Tingle.

"Play it again," said Buttercup.

"I'll try it with a third string now." Airy Fairy smiled. "I like this."

Binnnng. Bonnnng. Bunnnnng.

"Great," grinned all the other fairies.

All except Scary Fairy. She scowled. Airy Fairy was getting all the attention as usual.

"I'll try it with the bow now," said Airy Fairy.

That's when Scary Fairy saw her chance. She waved her little wand so that when Airy Fairy drew back her bow all the fairies near her fell over.

Their instruments clattered to the floor in a great CLANNNNNNG!!!

"Airy Fairy, be careful where you're sticking your elbow, you silly girl. You've knocked over all the others," said Miss Stickler.

"Oh dear, I didn't think I had touched... Oh dear, I don't remember bumping... Oh dear, sorry everyone. Sorry, Miss Stickler," said Airy Fairy.

Miss Stickler sighed, took the bow from Airy Fairy, and pointed her toward the French horn. "Go and try that," she said. "And try to keep out of trouble."

"Yes, Miss Stickler. Thank you, Miss Stickler," said Airy Fairy, and went over to the French horn.

It sat there looking very big and important.

"Hello, Mr. French Horn ... er, *bonjour*," said Airy Fairy nervously. "Do you mind if I play you?"

The French horn said nothing so Airy Fairy pressed one of its little keys.

24

Nothing happened. She tried another.
Still nothing happened.
She tried a third. Not
a sound.

"Oh dear," she said.
"I think this French horn
must be broken and
I've hardly touched it."

"You have to blow into it, you stupid fairy.
Don't you know anything?" sneered Scary
Fairy, who was by now showing off on the
violin.

"Oh, right," said Airy Fairy, and immediately blew into the fat end.

All the fairies fell down laughing.

"Blow into the mouthpiece at the other end, Airy Fairy, and stop fooling around," frowned Miss Stickler. "I never met a girl who fooled around this much when there was work to be done."

"Yes, Miss Stickler. Sorry, Miss Stickler. I didn't really think my mouth was big enough to blow into the big end."

The fairies giggled and Scary Fairy scowled.

Airy Fairy found the mouthpiece and had another quiet word with the French horn.

"You're probably tired coming all the way from France, Mr. Horn," she said, "but I'm just going to try giving you a little toot, if that's all right." And she blew into the mouthpiece. Nothing happened. She tried again. Still nothing happened. She tried a third time. Not a sound.

"Excuse me, Miss Stickler," said Airy Fairy. "But the French horn won't make a sound. I don't think it speaks any English."

Miss Stickler tutted and handed Airy Fairy the trombone instead. "Try this," she said. "And put some effort into it, Airy Fairy. Blow harder."

Airy Fairy really tried. She put the trombone to her lips and blew. Nothing happened. She puffed out her cheeks and blew harder still. Still nothing happened. Then, she took the deepest breath in the universe, and blew till her eyes grew enormous and her cheeks turned as red as bright apples. WHOOOOOOO.

Scary Fairy smiled slyly and waved her little wand. Suddenly, out of Airy Fairy's trombone came not sounds, but lots of light, frothy bubbles. They floated all around the fairies.

"Ooh," they gasped.

"Oh no," puffed Airy Fairy, as they reached Miss Stickler and burst with a POP on her pointed nose.

"Airy Fairy," Miss Stickler yelled. "You are here to get on with your work. You are here to learn to play an instrument for the welcome concert. You are not here to fool around doing silly spells."

"Oh, but I didn't. I mean, I haven't. I mean, I don't know anything about the bubbles."

But Miss Stickler wasn't listening. She took the trombone from Airy Fairy and handed her a violin. She stood over her.

"Put the violin under your chin," she said.

Airy Fairy did that.

"Hold the other end in your left hand."

Airy Fairy thought she did that.

"I said your left hand."

"Oh sorry, " said Airy Fairy, and changed hands.

"Take the bow in your right hand."

"Yes, Miss Stickler." Airy Fairy smiled. There was only one hand free now, so she knew which it was.

"And gently draw the bow across the strings."

Airy Fairy did that and a noise like a hundred hungry cats filled the room.

31

Miss Stickler sighed and raised her eyes to the ceiling.

"If this visit from Fairy Glissando wasn't so important to Fairy Gropplethorpe, Airy Fairy, I would ban you from going near a musical instrument ever again. However, you will persevere. Since you have fooled around all morning, you will not go out at break time, but will stay in and practice. Do you understand?"

"Yes, Miss Stickler." Airy Fairy was miserable. She liked break times best. She liked to sit out on the branches of the old oak tree and chat to her friends. Sometimes Macduff and Rainbow and the red squirrel came, too.

Airy Fairy sighed. "It's just Monday morning and already I'm in lots of trouble," she said to Buttercup and Tingle. "Surely the week can't get any worse."

"Oh yes, it can," muttered Scary Fairy slyly. "I'll soon see to that."

Chapter Three

But Airy Fairy was determined to try hard, so, next morning in class, when Miss Stickler started to draw some musical notes in the air, Airy Fairy paid close attention.

"This note is called a minim," said Miss Stickler, expertly whisking her wand. "Draw it carefully in your notebooks, Fairies, and remember what it looks like."

"Oh, that's the hard part," said Airy Fairy, picking up her pencil and sticking out her tongue. "How am I going to remember it's a minim when it looks like a backwards number six."

But she drew the note carefully and put its name beside it.

"Now this note's called a crotchet," said Miss Stickler, whisking her wand again. "Draw it carefully in your notebooks, Fairies, and remember what it looks like."

Airy Fairy looked at that note too, floating in the air, and sighed. "How am I going to remember it's a crotchet when it looks like a colored in, backwards number nine," she muttered. But she drew it carefully in her notebook and put its name beside it.

"We'll learn one more note this morning," said Miss Stickler, and whisked her wand and drew another note in the air.

"This note is called a quaver," she said. "Draw it carefully in your notebooks, Fairies, and remember what it looks like."

"Oh no," said Airy Fairy, chewing the end of her pencil. "How am I going to remember it's a quaver when it looks like a colored in, backwards number nine with a funny foot." But she drew it carefully in her notebook and put its name beside it. Then she sat back to look at what she'd done.

"Now, Fairies," said Miss Stickler. "While I mark your homework, you can have a few minutes to learn those notes by heart."

"Oh no," said Airy Fairy again. "I'm sure to get them all mixed up."

But then she had an idea. She went into her desk and rummaged among the old candy wrappers and broken pencils till she found a crumpled up piece of paper. She smoothed it out, and set to work writing down all the notes again. Then she added little extra bits to them.

"There," she smiled happily. "That will help me remember the names of all these notes, and Miss Stickler will be pleased."

And, when Miss Stickler wasn't looking, she showed what she'd done to Buttercup and Tingle.

"Good idea, Airy Fairy," they said, and giggled.

Scary Fairy looked over and frowned. "I wonder what they're up to," she muttered. "They always seem to be having fun." Then she saw Airy Fairy with the piece of paper. "I wonder what's on that?"

Quick as a flash, she waved her little wand and the piece of paper flew from Airy Fairy's hand and into hers.

"Oh no!" gasped Airy Fairy.

Scary Fairy looked at the piece of paper and smiled nastily. Then she waved her wand again and the paper sailed through the air and landed on the floor by Miss Stickler's desk.

Airy Fairy was aghast. Scary Fairy wasn't supposed to see that bit of paper and Miss Stickler certainly wasn't. She glared at Scary Fairy, slid out of her seat, and started to tiptoe toward the teacher's desk. *If only I can reach that bit of paper before Miss Stickler sees it,* she thought.

No chance. Scary Fairy smiled slyly, waved her little wand, and, all of a sudden, Airy Fairy's sneakers developed a very loud SQUEAK.

Miss Stickler looked up.

"Yes, what is it, Airy Fairy? Why aren't you at your desk learning your musical notes?"

"Er, … I am really, Miss Stickler," said Airy Fairy. "I just wrote them out again on another piece of paper to help me remember them, and the paper somehow floated out to your desk. I was just getting it."

Miss Stickler looked down and saw the piece of paper. "Is this it?" she asked, and picked it up.

Airy Fairy nodded miserably.

Miss Stickler looked at the paper and frowned. "If this is your idea of a joke, Airy Fairy…"

"No, it isn't," said Airy Fairy. "It really isn't. It was just to help me remember the names of the notes because I thought they all looked a bit like a backwards number six or number nine. I remember I used to draw my numbers that way when I was younger, and I thought I might have looked at them and got mixed up again, so I..."

Miss Stickler frowned again and held up her hand for silence. "Just explain to me, Airy Fairy, why the minim has grown two ears and a set of whiskers."

"I made it look a little like Minnie Mouse," said Airy Fairy miserably. "Minimouse," she added, in case Miss Stickler didn't understand.

Miss Stickler's frown deepened.

"Now explain to me why the crotchet is wearing a skirt and has my name beside it."

Airy Fairy gulped. She couldn't tell a lie. "Er, … well … sometimes … you can be a bit crotchety … with me." Then she added hastily, "When I've done something to annoy you."

The fairies were silent. They all felt so sorry for Airy Fairy. Except Scary Fairy, who was smiling and enjoying Airy Fairy's misery.

Miss Stickler looked at Airy Fairy. "And I suppose the quaver is drawn with a large hand and a walking stick to remind you..."

"That it gets a bit shaky and quavery, always hopping around on its one funny foot," explained Airy Fairy.

Miss Stickler sighed deeply. "I'll never understand, Airy Fairy, why you just can't learn things like the other fairies. Take this piece of paper back to your desk and just make sure that, whichever way you learn the notes, you learn them properly."

"Yes, Miss Stickler. Thank you, Miss Stickler," said Airy Fairy. She blew out her cheeks with relief, and went back to her desk.

On the way there, all the other fairies congratulated her.

"Great job, Airy Fairy," they said. "That's a really good way to remember the notes. We're going to do that, too." And they all began to put ears and whiskers on the minims in their notebooks.

Airy Fairy smiled at them, then stuck her tongue out at Scary Fairy as she passed her desk. Scary Fairy frowned. Things hadn't turned out quite the way she'd planned. Airy Fairy hadn't got into as much trouble as she hoped, and now she was more popular than ever.

"You've gotten away with things this time, Airy Fairy," she muttered. "But I haven't finished with you yet. Just you wait and see..."

Chapter Four

Later that day, the ten fairies all went back into the assembly hall to practice on the musical instruments they had chosen. Twink and Plink sat at the keyboard to play a duet. Honeysuckle blew into the French horn till her cheeks turned the color of scarlet beach balls. Silvie and Skelf tooted happily on the trumpets, while Cherri joined in with the tall, skinny trombone. Buttercup and Tingle played daintily on their violins, while Scary Fairy tried to drown out everyone else by playing loudly on the fat cello.

"Well done, Scary Fairy," beamed Miss Stickler. "That sounds wonderful. You really do play beautifully. Fairy Glissando is bound to be impressed."

Scary Fairy smirked. "But what about Airy Fairy, Aunt Stickler?" she said. "She's not practicing for the welcome concert. She's not playing anything at all."

Miss Stickler sighed. "Well, there's only a violin left, Airy Fairy," she said, "so you'll have to try that again."

"Yes, Miss Stickler," Airy Fairy blew out her cheeks and went to pick up the remaining violin.

She had just put it under her chin, the way Miss Stickler had shown her, when, *PING*, a string broke.

PING

"Oh," said Airy Fairy. "How did that happen? I never touched it."

She took the violin to Miss Stickler who replaced the string, tightening it around one of the little pegs on the neck of the violin.

"Now try to be more careful, Airy Fairy," she said.

"Yes, Miss Stickler," said Airy Fairy.

She laid her bow very gently across the strings and drew it across. *WHEEEAAAOW*.

Miss Stickler shuddered. "That's out of tune, Airy Fairy," she said. "Gently turn the peg and tighten that new string a little more."

Airy Fairy stretched her hand out toward the peg, which immediately popped out and fell at her feet.

"Oh," said Airy Fairy. "How did that happen? I never touched it."

She took the violin to Miss Stickler who sighed, replaced the peg, and tightened the string.

"I said *gently*, Airy Fairy," she said. "Gently draw your bow across the strings. You are trying to play the violin, not saw up wood for the fire."

"No, Miss Stickler. Thank you, Miss Stickler," said Airy Fairy and frowned. She was sure she hadn't touched the string or the peg. She looked across at Scary Fairy, who was playing away on the cello with a sly grin on her face.

"Hmm, I wonder," muttered Airy Fairy.

She put the violin under her chin again and very gently drew the bow across the strings. PING! PING! PING! PING! Every one of them snapped, flew up into the air and landed at Miss Stickler's feet.

"Airy Fairy!" she yelled.

HEE

HA

HA

HEE

HO

"Sorry, Miss Stickler. I really was gentle. I don't know how that happened." Then she looked across at Scary Fairy and saw her in a laughing fit ready to burst. "But I have a very good idea," she added under her breath.

HA

"I just don't think you're trying, Airy Fairy," stormed Miss Stickler. "Either that or you're deliberately trying to be difficult." And Miss Stickler was just in the middle of giving Airy Fairy a stern warning when Fairy Gropplethorpe appeared.

"Hello, Fairies," she said. "I just thought I'd pop in to see how you were all getting on with your musical instruments."

"Some people are getting on very well," said Miss Stickler, pointing to Scary Fairy.

"But some people don't seem to be trying at all." And she pointed to Airy Fairy.

Airy Fairy hung her head. "I'm sorry, Fairy Gropplethorpe. I just don't seem to be very musical."

"Perhaps she could just stand at the back and pretend to play when Fairy Glissando comes," suggested Miss Stickler. "Or, I could do a spell that would make her musical for an hour or two."

"No," Fairy Gropplethorpe shook her head. "That wouldn't be right. Everyone must do their best, even if it's not very good. It's the trying that's important."

"And we all know Airy Fairy can be very trying," sniffed Miss Stickler.

But Fairy Gropplethorpe wasn't listening. She had other news. "I've been examining the red coats the choir wears at Christmas time," she said. "I thought they might do for our little welcome concert, but they're looking a little shabby. So, if you all practice really hard and do your very best, you'll be allowed to magic up your own special fairy dress to wear to the concert."

"Ooh, fantastic," said the fairies. That was really special.

"I've always wanted to magic up my own dress," said Honeysuckle. "I think I might make mine dark blue with a silver moon, like the night sky."

"We'll do matching ones," said Twink and Plink. "Maybe in pale grey and pink, like a rosy dawn."

"Mine will have my own designer label attached," boasted Scary Fairy. "It'll say 'Scary Fairy Designs Ltd.' And I'm not saying what it will look like. I don't want anyone copying it."

Airy Fairy's forehead wrinkled in a worried frown. She had been the one in charge of magicking up the ten red coats for the choir, but had somehow magicked up ten red goats instead.

"Don't know what mine will look like," she whispered to Buttercup and Tingle.

Later, back in her bedroom, she told Rainbow and Macduff all that had happened that day.

"But how am I going to practice playing the violin with Scary Fairy messing it up every time?" she said. "And if Fairy Gropplethorpe thinks I'm not trying hard, I'll be the only fairy at the welcome concert not wearing a special dress. I'll be the only one standing there in my old school uniform. What am I going to do?"

Rainbow and Macduff came and leaned on Airy Fairy's legs. They knew she was unhappy, but they didn't know what to do about it.

Chapter Five

Airy Fairy was determined to try hard. She didn't want to let Fairy Gropplethorpe down, so she thought of a plan.

"I'll set my alarm clock for extra early," she said to Rainbow and Macduff, "and tomorrow morning, while everyone else is still asleep, I'll go down to the assembly hall and have a really good practice on the violin. That's bound to help."

Rainbow meowed and Macduff woofed. It sounded like a good plan.

Airy Fairy made sure her little alarm clock was properly wound up before she pulled on her pink fairy pajamas and climbed into bed with pocket Ted.

"Good night, Rainbow. Good night, Macduff. Good night, pocket Ted," she said, and fell fast asleep. After a while, she began to dream. She dreamed about the kind of special dress she would like to wear to the

concert. A pale green one with strands of pink rose petals floated by.

Oh, that looks nice, dreamed Airy Fairy.

Then a lemon one with orange sugar buttons floated by.

Oh, that looks nice too, dreamed Airy Fairy.

The lemon dress was followed by a soft, silky, lavender one with frosted white lace on the collar and cuffs.

Oh, they all look so pretty, I can't decide,
dreamed Airy Fairy ... then didn't have
to when her little alarm clock went
DRINNNNG, and woke her up.

Airy Fairy sat up with a start. "Where did
all those lovely dresses go?" she muttered,
looking down at her pink fairy pajamas.
Then she remembered about the music
practice. She got up, put on her fairy
slippers, slipped into her bathrobe, and

popped pocket Ted into the pocket. Then, followed by a sleepy Rainbow and Macduff, she slipped out of her bedroom and headed for the stairs.

"It's very dark," she whispered to the pets. "I should have brought a flashlight. I can't see a thing."

She was right. She didn't see the trailing belt of her bathrobe till she tripped over it and skidded all the way downstairs.

WHUMP! She landed at the bottom. Rainbow and Macduff scurried after her, their paws click-clicking on the wooden stairs.

"Oh," puffed Airy Fairy. "I've never come downstairs that way before." She checked that pocket Ted was safe, then sat for a moment to catch her breath and to listen. "But we're all right," she whispered. "We can go on into the assembly hall. Nobody heard us."

But someone had. Someone had opened her bedroom door and was also listening. That someone frowned, put on her bathrobe, and began to follow Airy Fairy. That someone was determined to find out what was happening. That someone was Scary Fairy.

Airy Fairy went into the assembly hall, flew up onto the platform, and picked up a violin. She put it under her chin, and, by the light of the moon, now sliding out from behind a cloud, she began to play very softly and gently. Rainbow and Macduff put their paws up to their ears, then put them down again. Actually, Airy Fairy's playing didn't sound too bad, so they sat and waited while she practiced and practiced.

Outside the assembly hall door, Scary Fairy frowned again before smiling slyly and settling down to wait.

Airy Fairy kept on practicing till the moon went in and the sun came out. Then she stopped and gave a great yawn.

"Come on, Rainbow. Come on, Macduff," she whispered. "Time to go back to sleep." And with the pets at her heels she tiptoed quietly back to her bedroom.

Then out from the shadows stepped Scary Fairy. She flew over to the platform and waved her wand. She stood for a moment and looked at the result of her spell. "That should get Airy Fairy into plenty of trouble," she snickered, and went back to bed.

Back in her bedroom, Airy Fairy smiled sleepily at Rainbow and Macduff. "My playing really wasn't too bad, was it?" she said. "Maybe I'll get to play in the welcome concert after all. Perhaps I'll even get to magic myself up a fantastic new dress, though I don't think I've got any chance of playing with Fairy Glissando. Scary Fairy really is the most musical fairy. But at least I won't be letting Fairy Gropplethorpe down, and Miss Stickler won't be able to say I'm not trying, will she?"

No, she wouldn't. Miss Stickler would be able to say something much, much worse.

Chapter Six

Later that morning, Airy Fairy skipped along to the assembly hall for music practice.

Miss Stickler's bound to be pleased when she hears me play today, she thought.

But Miss Stickler didn't look pleased. In fact, her face was grim as she went up onto the platform and turned to face the fairies.

"Someone was down here in this hall during the night," she said, "and I demand to know who that someone was."

Airy Fairy was amazed. *How did Miss Stickler find out?* she wondered. Did teachers really know everything?

Airy Fairy couldn't tell a lie. She put up her hand. "I was here in the night," she said. "I came down to..."

But before she could explain, Miss Stickler whipped aside the stage curtain. "Then you are the one responsible for this!"

Airy Fairy gasped, as did all the other fairies. The new musical instruments were lying all over the floor, smashed to pieces.

"Oh no!" Airy Fairy was shocked. "I didn't... I mean, I would never... I..."

"Then who else?" asked Miss Stickler. "You were the only one here, Airy Fairy. You've admitted it. It must have been you."

"She probably smashed the instruments so that no one could play at the concert, and she wouldn't look so hopeless," sniffed Scary Fairy.

Miss Stickler nodded. "Fairy Gropplethorpe has gone to meet Fairy Glissando, so I shall try to repair the instruments before they get back. Meanwhile, you, Airy Fairy, are banned from taking part in the concert and banned from magicking up a new dress."

Airy Fairy couldn't believe it. "But I really, really didn't..." she started to say.

But Miss Stickler wasn't listening. "Go to your room, Airy Fairy. I'll deal with you later."

All the fairies were silent as Airy Fairy trailed miserably out of the assembly hall and upstairs to her bedroom. Only Scary Fairy smirked. "Serves her right. She's such an idiot."

Airy Fairy sat on her bed with pocket Ted and gazed unhappily out of her window. The red squirrel passed by and peeped in, but even seeing him couldn't cheer her up. After a while she saw Fairy Gropplethorpe arrive with Fairy Glissando, and she heard the music start up and the welcome concert begin.

"Miss Stickler must have managed to fix the instruments," she said to Rainbow and Macduff. "But you know I didn't smash them up, don't you?"

Rainbow came and sat on her lap and Macduff snuggled up close to her side. Then Rainbow began to meow.

"What is it?" asked Airy Fairy. "Are you hungry?"

Rainbow meowed louder, jumped off Airy Fairy's lap, and went to the door.

"Oh," said Airy Fairy. "I'm supposed to stay in my room, but I suppose it would be all right to go down to the kitchen to feed you. Everyone else will be too busy."

Airy Fairy and the pets tiptoed downstairs past the assembly hall and into the kitchen. Airy Fairy went to the big cupboard where Fairy Gropplethorpe kept the cans of pet food and opened a can for Rainbow and another for Macduff. Then, while they ate, she sat and listened to the music coming from the hall. It sounded good and her feet started to tap. Without thinking, she picked up a couple of wooden spoons from the kitchen table and began drumming on some pet food cans ... then on some empty jam jars ... then on some pots and pans.

Rainbow and Macduff finished their food, picked up their paws, and began to dance.

"Hey, you two are really good," smiled Airy Fairy. And, as the pets danced, she began to drum louder and louder. BOOM BANGA BOOM BANGA BOOM BOOM BOOM.

She was so busy drumming, she didn't notice that the music from the hall had stopped, and she didn't notice that the kitchen door had opened, and she certainly didn't notice that a small crowd had gathered, till…

"Airy Fairy, what are you doing?" yelled Miss Stickler.

"Why, she's making music, of course," said a tall stranger, who could only be Fairy Glissando. "But why wasn't she in the assembly hall?"

"Yes." Fairy Gropplethorpe frowned. "I thought when you said Airy Fairy was confined to her room that perhaps she had a bad cold..."

Miss Stickler took a deep breath. "I wanted to spare you the awful details, Fairy Gropplethorpe," she said, and told her what had happened. "Airy Fairy denies it, of course. But she was the only one in the assembly hall last night, so she must have smashed up the instruments."

"I didn't, Fairy Gropplethorpe," said Airy Fairy. "I got up extra early to practice for the concert because I wasn't very good. Rainbow and Macduff and I tiptoed downstairs to the hall, but I didn't smash up the instruments. I really didn't."

"Hmm." Fairy Gropplethorpe called Rainbow and Macduff to her, then she bent down and touched her magic wand to their heads.

TELL ME TRULY,
TELL ME RIGHT,
ALL THAT HAPPENED IN
THE NIGHT

"Airy Fairy tripped on the belt of her bathrobe and slid all the way downstairs on her bottom," woofed Macduff.

"Then she practiced the violin for ages, and went back to bed," meowed Rainbow.

The fairies started to giggle. Fairy Gropplethorpe tapped the heads of the pets with her wand again.

"Rainbow and Macduff cannot lie," she said, "and I don't think Airy Fairy is lying either. Smashing things up quietly so no one will hear is a very hard spell to do, and we all know that Airy Fairy's not very good at spelling."

Airy Fairy smiled with relief. For once it was good to be terrible at spelling.

"No," went on Fairy Gropplethorpe, "whoever did this is someone who is very good at spelling. Very good indeed. I wonder who that could be?"

Everyone was silent. Everyone knew it had to be Scary Fairy, but she was pretending to look out of the window and was saying nothing.

"However, we have no proof," went on Fairy Gropplethorpe, "and no one should ever be accused of anything without proof."

"That's right," said Fairy Glissando. "Now, I really enjoyed the welcome concert, but since Airy Fairy didn't get a chance to play, and since she really impressed me with the music she made on her makeshift drums, I think she should join me in a little rock concert." And she magicked herself up a fantastic multicolored rock guitar. "Now, Airy Fairy," she said, "let's make some music."

"Just one thing first," said Fairy Gropplethorpe. "I think we have to make it up to Airy Fairy for wrongly accusing her," and she waved her wand and changed Airy Fairy's old school uniform into a sparkly silver dress that shimmered with a thousand tiny lights.

"Wow," said the fairies. "Just look at Airy Fairy. She's a real rock chick now."

Only Scary Fairy, her face like a mean, black thundercloud, wouldn't look at Airy Fairy.

Airy Fairy was too happy to notice. "Thank you for the dress, Fairy Gropplethorpe," she breathed, giving it a little twirl. "It's lovely."

Fairy Gropplethorpe smiled and nodded. Then a wonderful sound filled the room as Fairy Glissando's fingers flew up and down the neck of her guitar. "Ready to join me in some magic music now, Airy Fairy?" she asked.

"I certainly am." Airy Fairy grinned, and picked up her wooden spoons.

BOOM BANGA BOOM BOOM BANG...